One for the Price of Two

Retold by Cynthia Jameson

Pictures by Anita Lobel

Parents' Magazine Press / New York

Library of Congress Cataloging in Publication Data
Jameson, Cynthia.
    One for the price of two.

    SUMMARY: An old Japanese man brags so much about
his fine heifer, the master clog maker and his apprentice
decide to teach him a lesson.

    I. Lobel, Anita, illus. II. Title.
PZ7.J1560n   [E]   72-705
ISBN 0-8193-0602-9
ISBN 0-8193-0603-7 (lib bdg.)

Especially for Christiane

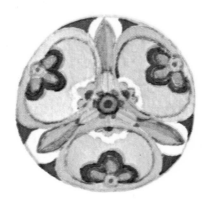

Long years ago in ancient Japan, there lived
an old man who was known by the name of Kichei.
One crisp autumn morning Kichei left his village
and set out for town to buy himself a heifer.

Arriving at the marketplace, he soon came upon one small, fawn-colored heifer with large, chocolate-brown eyes. So pretty was she that the very sight of her gladdened the old man's heart. All at once the owner appeared.

"Buy that heifer, my friend, and you'll never regret it," he declared. "For there's not another like her in the whole world!"

And, as was the custom in the marketplaces
of old Japan, the owner took Kichei's hand into
his kimono sleeve and pressed several fingers
against the old man's palm.
In this manner, he let Kichei know the price he
asked while keeping it a secret from
other buyers.

Once they had settled on a price, Kichei
counted out the coins and proudly led his new
purchase away. Now Kichei decided to call
on his old friend, the master clog maker.
Hah! How envious he will be when he sees my
beautiful heifer! thought Kichei, hustling the
little animal toward the clog shop.

"Kichei San! What a surprise," greeted the
master warmly. "And what a fine-looking heifer."
Tethering the little one to the gatepost,
Kichei hurried into the shop.
"Today good fortune smiled upon me," he began.
"I came to market to buy an ordinary
heifer and instead found that priceless creature."
Bending closer to the clog maker, he added in a
half-whisper, "You see, there's not another
heifer like her in the whole world!"
On and on babbled the old man until his boasting
tired the ears of his friend. As it happened,
the master had a clever apprentice named Iosakitzi.
All the while that Kichei kept up his chatter,
the apprentice was busily painting clogs and
listening with one ear.

When the old visitor slipped out for a moment
to buy some tobacco, Iosakitzi spoke up.
"Master, Kichei San wears us thin with his
bragging. If you promise to reward me,
I'll teach him a little lesson by stealing his
heifer while he leads it home."
"Impossible!" chuckled the master clog maker.
"You may be sure that Kichei San will guard her
with his life."
"But I know a way, Master," insisted the
apprentice. "That is, if the reward is great
enough . . ."
At this, the master smiled. "Well and good! If
you steal Kichei San's heifer without his seeing
you, I'll pay you twice your day's work."

"Agreed!" exclaimed the apprentice.
With flying fingers he finished his work.
Then, taking a new pair of clogs, he left the
shop and sped down the road that led
through the dense grove of ginkgo trees. For
Iosakitzi knew that this was the way the
old man would take to go home.

Later, back at the clog shop, Kichei saw
that it was time to leave. He rose from his
silk floor cushion and bid his friend farewell.

It was not long before he and his heifer arrived
at the grove of ginkgo trees and turned in
along a narrow path. Suddenly Kichei spied
something lying in the middle of the path. It
caught the rays of the sun and gleamed with great
brightness. Drawing nearer, he saw that it was
a fine, new, not-yet-walked-in clog!
"Oya!" he exclaimed with delight.
He was about to pick it up, but a thought made
him stop.
"Yo! What would I do with just *one* clog? I have
two feet."
And so, with his thoughts still on the clog, the
old man went on.

When he had gone but a short distance, his eyes
caught the gleam of another new clog lying
in the path—just as before! The old man
recognized it as the mate to the first, and he

whistled with glee and hopped up and down on
one leg.

"Truly this is my day of good fortune. The gods
want me to have *two* new clogs—one for each foot!"
The old peasant tied the heifer, hurried back
to fetch the first clog, and returned with it to
the tree where he had left the heifer.

But to his great surprise she was gone! Rubbing
his eyes in disbelief, he rushed about in circles
and called at the top of his voice.

"Little one, where are you? *Chu-chu-chu.*"
The shadows of late afternoon were growing
longer, and still there was no sign of the little lost
heifer. Filled with despair, the old man trudged
back to town, forgetting all about his new-found,
not-yet-walked-in clogs. By this time, Iosakitzi
had already returned to the clog shop with the
heifer and was receiving his reward.

It wasn't long before there came a rapping at
the shop door.

"Kichei San!" the master exclaimed, feigning
surprise. "What brings you back?"

The old peasant entered, and his face was troubled
as he explained that he had lost his heifer.

"Now I shall have to buy another, and," he

concluded miserably, "there's not another like her."
"What bad fortune," sighed the master. "Of course
if you want another heifer I could sell you mine."
"*Your* heifer!" Kichei cried. "I did not know
that you owned a heifer."
No sooner said, than in strode the apprentice
Iosakitzi with a heifer at his side.

Arching his brow, the old man looked closely at
the animal and said to the master, "What is
your price?"

"The same that you paid at market," came the reply.

"What?" flared the old man. "Why, that heifer
was far better-looking than this one. Surely you
cannot expect me to pay the same price!"

"Are you sure the first heifer was better-looking?"
demanded the master with a smile.

"Of course!" replied Kichei firmly. "You forget,
I am an expert on animals."

At length the two friends agreed on a price, and the old man's heart was happy as he set out for his village with the new heifer. And behind the windows of the clog shop, master and apprentice howled with laughter.

Finally, Iosakitzi was able to speak.
"Master, Kichei San is more foolish than
I thought. Let me steal his heifer once more."
"Go ahead, then," replied the master. "But be
careful. This time he will be on his guard."
Now, with a burst of speed, Iosakitzi dashed
along a hidden forest path and reached the grove
of ginkgo trees before Kichei arrived.

He hid himself behind the fan-shaped leaves
and waited. As soon as he heard the old man's voice
and the clickety-clack of hooves, the apprentice
began to low.

 M-*m-o-o-o* . . .   M-*m-o-o-o* . . .

The old man halted and listened. Once more came
the sweet, melancholy sound.

 M-*m-o-o-o* . . .

"My lost heifer!" Kichei cried. "She has come back."
Without another thought, the old man secured his
second heifer to a branch and bounded off in search
of the first.

But the longer Kichei looked, the farther away
he wandered. At the same time, Iosakitzi
was stealthily circling round to the tree where
the heifer stood. In a flash, he undid the rope
and trotted the little animal back to the
clog shop.

As dusk drew nigh, Kichei gave up all hope
of finding his lost heifer and returned to the tree
to fetch the second. Imagine the old man's
dismay when he discovered that the *second*
heifer had now disappeared!

"Aiyie!" he wailed.

Swiftly his eyes searched the trees, but darkness
was already closing in.

Now there was nothing left but to return to town
and pour out his misfortune to his good friend.
And, in due time, he was in the clog shop recount-
ing his sad tale.

At length the master said thoughtfully, "Old
friend, I may be able to help you yet." So saying,
he clapped his hands, and in walked Iosakitzi
with a small, pretty heifer. At this sight the old
man was speechless.

"And now, Kichei San," continued the master,
"I am willing to sell you this fine heifer at half price."
Slowly the old man's eyes moved . . . from the animal
. . . to the face of the master . . . to the face
of the apprentice . . .

Suddenly he burst into laughter, and in the next moment the other two were laughing with him. "Ho!" he gasped. "What a joke on me! I would have bought my own heifer a third time over if I had not noticed how you two were winking at each other."

Then, to show that he bore them no ill will, Kichei invited the master and apprentice to supper at his house. And so, in the pale light of the moon, the three set out, leading a very pretty but very tired little heifer on her final trek home.

Cynthia Jameson began writing at an early age and has always been interested in stories for children. She is the author of *Catofy the Clever*, recently published for children six to nine, and *The Clay Pot Boy* and *Winter Hut*, soon to be published.

Anita Lobel is the illustrator of *The Wishing Penny*, *The Wisest Man in the World*, and *How the Tsar Drinks Tea*, all three published by Parents' Magazine Press. Among the many other beautiful picture books she has illustrated is *Little John*, a first-prize winner in the *Book World's* 1972 Spring Festival. And, of course, Mrs. Lobel writes as well as illustrates for children, as does her husband, Arnold Lobel.

The Lobels and their two children, Adrienne and Adam, live in Brooklyn.